A Merry Mersey Christmas

A Merry Mersey Christmas

(or, who killed Santa Claus?)
A Short Story

Brian L. Porter

From the Author

A Merry Mersey Christmas has been written in response to reader requests for a special Christmas story revolving around Detective Inspector Andy Ross and the Merseyside Police, Specialist Murder Investigation Squad. Not an easy task to condense a full-blown murder mystery into a short story, but, as my thanks to all those who continue to support the series, here's a special story to celebrate the team, and to wish a Happy Christmas to all my readers, for Christmas 2018. I hope you enjoy this rather more light-hearted tale of an unusual crime that takes place three days before Christmas. Can Ross, Izzie Drake and the team solve the murder of a Department Store Santa Claus in time to have Christmas Day off? Let's see, shall we?

The Mersey Mystery Series

You don't need to have read any of the books in the series in order to enjoy this short story, but if you'd like to take a look at the novels in the series, please go to http://getbook.at/MerseyMysteries.

Books in the series:

A Mersey Killing

All Saints, Murder on the Mersey

A Mersey Maiden

A Mersey Mariner

A Very Mersey Murder

Last Train to Lime Street

The Mersey Monastery Murders (Coming soon)

Special Note

You will find a reference in this story to 'bizzies'. For those unfamiliar with the local vocabulary in Liverpool, the word is an old slang term, simply meaning, the police.

Contents

1   The Call   1

2   The Body   3

3   The Witnesses   9

4   Good Santa, Bad Santa   17

5   Merry Christmas   22

The Author   28

Chapter 1

The Call

"You're kidding me, surely? Is this a wind-up? It's three days before Christmas." Andy Ross almost shouted down the phone, in response to a call from the control room at Merseyside Police Headquarters, to his home. It was eight-thirty in the evening, the date was December 22nd, and he and his wife, Maria were about to sit down to a late evening meal, having spent an hour wrapping presents for relatives and friends.

"It's no joke, D.I. Ross," Jenny, the control room supervisor assured him. "The call was confirmed by the officer on the scene."

"But the victim. That can't be real, can it?"

"Afraid so, and as you are the senior officer on call, you get the pleasure of responding. I've also called Sergeant Drake and she said to tell you she'll meet you there."

"And just where is, there?" Ross inquired, as he realised Jenny still hadn't given him a location for the crime.

"Pearson's Emporium," she replied. "It's that new cheap department store that opened in the old closed down bank on..."

"I know where it is, thanks, Jenny."

"I'll leave it with you then, shall I? Just make sure there isn't a double-parked sled with half a dozen reindeer attached when you get there," she joked.

"Okay, I'm convinced. I'll be there asap," Ross confirmed. As he placed the phone back in its place on the cradle, in its place on the hall table, close to the front door of his home in Prescot, a few miles from Liverpool City Centre, Maria appeared through the door from the lounge.

"Not a call-out, surely?" she looked disappointed, but resigned to the fact this was all part of her husband's job.

"Sorry, but yes. You'll never believe it," he hesitated before continuing. He had a wry smile on his face, unusual considering his evening had just been disrupted.

"Go on, spit it out," said Maria, "What won't I believe?"

Unable to contain himself, Andy Ross took hold of his wife, one hand on each shoulder, and pulled her , him, gave her a short but loving kiss and whispered in her ear, "Someone just killed Santa Claus!"

"Andy, don't play silly buggers with me. Come on, what's happened to drag you out at this time of night?"

"I just told you. Someone killed Santa," he looked her in the eyes and Maria could tell he was deadly serious.

"You mean it, don't you?"

"Yes, looks like someone knocked off the department store Santa at that low-price department store, Pearson's Emporium, in town."

Ross took his mobile phone from its place on the charger in their bedroom as he extricated his warm, camel-coloured overcoat that Maria had bought him a couple of Christmases ago, and dropped the phone into one of its deep pockets. He picked up his brown leather gloves, added a pair of black leather shoes, a real mismatch with his coat and gloves and was out of the door and in his car within ten minutes of receiving the call from headquarters.

Chapter 2

The Body

Pearson's Emporium was typical of many of the stores of similar status that were opening in towns and cities all over the country, as many old, established stores ceased trading in the current economic downturn, to be replaced by others, operating on shoestring budgets and miniscule margins, usually on short leases. These businesses would usually operate profitably as long as they could remain economically viable, before their owners would close the doors one last time and move on to pastures new.

It was almost 9.20 pm by the time Ross pulled up outside the entrance to the store, where he parked on the double yellow lines immediately outside the store's double plate glass doors. He was confident there were no traffic wardens on duty at that time of night so he was safe from receiving a parking ticket. He immediately saw that his sergeant, Clarissa (Izzie) Drake was already on the premises, as her car was parked a few yards further along the street. She'd conveniently left the space nearest the doors for her boss.

Andy Ross was the operational head of Merseyside Police's Specialist Murder Investigation Team, set up to investigate strange or unusual cases that fell outside the normal purview of the regular C.I.D. section of the force. Izzie Drake had been his sergeant and partner for enough years that the pair had developed an almost telepathic working relationship, and it was thought by those who knew them well that they could almost read one another's minds. Together with their team of highly qualified, expert detectives, the best of the best, as Ross called them, they had been responsible for the apprehension and arrest of some of the most dangerous and devious murderers the force had faced over the previous ten years.

Ross was met at the front doors of the store by two uniformed officers, both constables, and Ross assumed there were others inside, as evidenced by the presence of two police Peugeot vehicles also parked close to the store entrance. Ross held up his warrant card as he walked up to the constables, identifying himself and unfastening his coat as the heat of the store interior brought him out in an instant sweat.

Constable Roger Dixon informed Ross that Sergeant Drake was already on the second floor of the building, together with Constables Greig and Forsyth, where Santa's Grotto was located. Dixon also confirmed that since their arrival, he and Constable Newton, assuming that a murder may have taken place, had forbidden anyone from leaving the building and that staff and customers alike were waiting to be interviewed in the store's restaurant, located on the top floor. They were currently being supervised by the store's two security guards, until more police units arrived.

Izzie was waiting for him as he exited the lift on the second floor and made his way to the grotto, which was located immediately in front of him, in the middle of the shop floor where it would be unmissable by eager children as they walked out of the lift with their parents.

"Not what we expected this close to Christmas, is it?" she said as she led him into the grotto through a silver, tinsel covered archway, guarded by two elves, dressed in gaudy red and green costumes. They were electrically powered automatons which would normally spend the store's opening hours nodding their heads and issuing recorded voices welcoming visitors to Santa's Grotto. Ross inwardly thanked God for small mercies that they had been turned off when the store closed at 8 pm even though, standing there, inanimate, with their fixed grins in place, they did have a rather scary, unnerving appearance.

"Definitely not," Ross agreed as he followed her into the grotto. Two constables nodded in greeting as he walked past them with Drake. There, in the centre of the brightly decorated Christmas scene, made to look like Santa's workshop at the North Pole, was a large, red velvet upholstered throne, upon which the unmistakable figure of a man dressed in a traditional Santa suit, appeared, to the casual observer, to have fallen asleep with his head drooped forward, his bearded chin resting on his amply padded chest.

"What have we got then, Izzie?" he asked, assuming she'd already found out some basic information before his arrival.

"Santa, aka Daniel Thomas, was found like this shortly before closing time. The grotto hadn't had any visitors in the previous half hour and the floor manager came to tell Danny, as he was known, to pack up and knock off for the night. When he failed to receive a reply from Danny, he thought at first the man had fallen asleep and he stepped forward, meaning to give him a shale and a mild rebuke. As Mr. Revitt, the floor manager says, Danny was almost seventy and he wouldn't have been too hard on him. Unfortunately, when he drew closer to Santa, he saw this."

Izzie took Ross by the arm and guided him to the side of Santa's throne, where she pointed out a vicious-looking knife, buried deep into the old man's neck. There was clearly no chance this was an accident, Ross surmised.

"Ah," said Ross. "Someone obviously didn't like poor old Santa."

"You can say that again," Drake nodded in agreement. I think our problem lies in the fact nobody knows when it happened. The killer might still be in the store or could have left anytime since 7.15 pm, which was the last recorded kiddie visit to the Grotto."

"So our killer could be miles away or might be sitting upstairs sipping tea or coffee while we're trying to work this out," said Ross. "I hoped we might not need them, but I think we have to get some of the team in here to carry out initial interviews with the people upstairs."

"Agreed," said Drake, "I'll get on the phone and summon them. Who do you want, Boss?"

"Derek McLennan, Tony Curtis and Sam Gable should be enough for now. It's a shame Sofie's at home in Germany," he referred to the team's on-loan German detective, Sofie Meyer." How many people have we got in the restaurant?"

"Forty two, but most of them are staff. Only sixteen customers were left in the store when the body was discovered at 7.45."

"Right, get D.C. Devenish in too. These two fine lads can assist by taking initial statements and the names and addresses of those still on the premises," Ross decided, indicating the two constables who at that moment in time were as much use as the two elves at the grotto entrance.

A pinging sound announced the arrival of the lift and as the doors opened, out stepped the rotund and always overweight senior medical examiner, Doctor William Nugent, closely followed by his cadaverous assistant, Francie Lees, who members of Ross's team privately joked looked more dead than some of the poor souls he and his boss worked upon in the mortuary. Nugent himself, an expert in his field, was known as Fat Willie to the detectives, though the name was never mentioned outside the murder team's squad room.

Nugent strode across the shop floor towards the grotto with Lees trailing in his wake, looking weighed down by the two cameras and a heavy case of camera and forensic equipment draped over his shoulders, looking heavy enough to dislocate the poor man's arms. He looked as miserable as usual and for some reason, wore a red and white Santa hat, totally out of place on Lees head, especially considering the circumstances.

"Inspector Ross, Sergeant Drake, season's greeting to the pair of ye," Nugent boomed, displaying just a hint of his native Glaswegian accent. He'd left Glasgow over twenty years previously but the accent was never far away, and always grew stronger when he was stressed or flustered.

"You too, Doc," Ross replied. "Like your hat, Mr. Lees," he added with a note of sarcasm in his voice.

Lees mumbled something in reply which Ross failed to catch, and he looked inquiringly towards Nugent.

"Ah, the hat," he smiled. "Young Francis is wearing it for a bet. One of my colleagues said he'd donate a hundred pounds to a charity of Francis's choice if he'd wear that monstrous looking hat on every call out we received during the advent season, so he's only a couple of days to go and the RSPCC will be receiving a nice sum for Christmas.

"Very noble of you, Mr. Lees," don't you agree, Izzie? Ross relented a little towards Lees.

"Oh yes. I'm sure the children's charity will be grateful to you for the contribution." Drake replied.

"Oh no, he'll be donating the money anonymously," Nugent added.

"What? You'll have made yourself look a right plonker all month and you don't even want them to know who the money's come from?"

Lees just smiled sardonically in reply.

Ross shook his head in wonder. "Ah, well it takes all sorts," he said, closing the interlude of the hat.

"Now, what do we have here?" Nugent asked of no-one in particular, as he began his examination of the body of Danny Thomas. "Ah," he said after a minute or so. "I'd say you're safe to assume the poor fellow expired as a result of the nasty stab wound in his neck," he ventured.

"What? An opinion in advance of the autopsy? Are you feeling alright, Doc?" Ross was grinning as he spoke.

"Very funny, D. I. Ross. Even I can make a reasonable prophesy based on yon evil-looking weapon sticking out of poor old Santa's neck."

"His name's Daniel Thomas, aged 65, I'm told," Ross pointed out.

"Aye, well, he's Santa to me, and that thing in his neck is no professional hit man's weapon. It looks like a kitchen knife to me. I'll be certain when I remove it of course." Nugent replied.

Another ping from the lift announced the arrival of the leader of the forensics team, Miles Booker and four of this technicians, each loaded down with whatever equipment they felt they'd need based on the information they'd received.

"All yours, Miles," said Ross. "Me and my lot will be on the next floor up, talking with potential witnesses."

"Where are your lot?" Booker asked as he looked around and saw not a single member of Ross's investigative team, aside of course, from Izzie Drake.

"On their way, I hope," Ross replied, looking at Drake for confirmation as she walked towards him.

"Well?" he asked.

"On their way," she responded.

Chapter 3

The Witnesses

"And you never met Mr. Thomas before you hired him to be your Santa Claus?" Ross asked Edwin Pearson, the proprietor and hands-on manager of the emporium.

"That's right. I interviewed a few, maybe twenty applicants and Danny was just right for the job. He seemed naturally friendly, funny and jolly, just what you expect from Santa Claus, if you know what I mean."

Ross nodded. "Did you do any checks on his suitability, check references etc?"

"Of course, and he had to pass the police background check before he was allowed to work closely with children. He's done the job before in a couple of stores in the city."

"No complaints from anyone since he's been here? No customers making accusations against him, no fall-outs with other members of staff?"

"No, Danny was a good man, as far as I could see. No complaints, always on time and really got on well with the kids who came to see him."

The rest of Ross's team were hard at work talking to staff members, and the few customers who'd been in the store at the estimated time of Santa's death. Not all of them had been on the second floor at the time of the murder and so could quickly be eliminated as suspects. The first break in the case came as D.C. Lenny (Tony) Curtis, so-called because of his remarkable resemblance to the old movie idol of that name spoke to a woman who was trying very aggressively to get someone to listen to her.

"Will one of you people please listen to me?" she shouted. "My little girl needs to be home in bed. She has to be up early for school tomorrow, and she saw who killed Santa!"

Having just finished talking to an unhelpful toy department employee, Curtis immediately walked up to the woman, both hands held upward in a placatory gesture.

"Madam, I'm Detective Constable Curtis. Please, calm down. Come and sit down," he led her to the area where chairs had been provided so the police could conduct their interviews in some degree of comfort. "You say your daughter saw the killer?"

"Yes, she saw the bloody killer. I've been trying to tell someone for the last half hour but nobody wants to hear what my Maisie has to say, because she's only ten years old. But I'm telling you, she doesn't tell lies."

"Okay, okay," Curtis did his best to calm the woman down. "And your name is?"

"Carrie, Carrie Poole, and this is my daughter, Maisie," she indicated her daughter, a small, blonde-haired girl, thin, but not underfed, clutching a large teddy bear in her arms, with store labels attached. Curtis wondered if the girl and her mother were either very clever, or very stupid shoplifters.

"Hello Maisie," Curtis began, in as friendly a voice as he could manage. He wasn't used to interviewing little girls of Maisie's age. "That's a lovely teddy bear. Is it yours?"

"Don't be silly," Maisie replied. "I'm ten, not two. I'm too old for teddies. This is a Christmas present for my little sister, Susie."

"Ah, I see," said Curtis, feeling a little guilty for thinking the worst of Maisie's mum. "And where's Susie now?"

"She's at home with my Dad. She's too young to come shopping with Me and Mum. She's three."

Feeling he'd done enough to calm Maisie enough to ask her some pertinent questions, he went for it.

"Now, Maisie, your Mum says you saw who attacked Santa. Is that right?"

"Yes, but Mum didn't believe me at first."

"But she does now. Is that right?"

Carrie Poole nodded as Maisie replied, "Yes. She knows I don't tell lies."

"So tell me, please, Maisie," Curtis took a deep breath, wondering just what was coming next, "who attacked Santa?"

"Santa," was Maisie's one word reply.

"Yes, someone attacked Santa, I know that," said Curtis, "But who was it who you saw attacking him?"

"Santa," Maisie repeated. "It was the *other* Santa."

Curtis suddenly felt a tingle run down his spine. This little girl might have really seen something relevant.

"What other Santa would that be, Maisie?" he asked, keeping his voice as quiet and even as he could.

"I'm not silly," she said, and then, keeping her own voice quiet and in an almost conspiratorial tone, so other children couldn't hear her, she went on, "I know Santa isn't real, you know, but it's nice that the little children believe in him, isn't it? Anyway, Santa was sitting in his chair, but thee were no kids waiting to go in to see him. Then the other Santa came up to him. I thought he must be his friend, or that the shop had, like, two Santas, you know? One to work while the other one rested. They're really old you know, and must need lots of sleep," Maisie said in a knowing voice. "They must be at least thirty or forty, like you," or even older.

Curtis fought back a smile or a wry remark. He was thirty-one, felt more like twenty-one, and here was a ten year-old who obviously saw people of his age group as ancient enough to be Santa Claus! He felt he needed to bring Maisie's mum into the conversation.

"Mrs Poole, did you see this other Santa?"

"Well, yes, but I didn't take any notice of him. It was just a fleeting glance of a man in a red Santa suit as he headed through the double doors that lead to the stairs over there," she pointed, her information being useless as far as Curtis was concerned, except for perhaps giving the police an indication of how the killer departed after knifing Danny Thomas. He tried again with Maisie.

Even the young child seemed to realise the idiocy of his question and Maisie rolled her eyes as she replied, "Yes, A big, fat man, in a red and white Santa suit and a fake white beard, wearing black boots."

"Yes, of course. Daft question wasn't it?"

"Yes, it was," Maisie spoke with the innocence of youth in her voice.

"Okay, let's try something else. Did you see what this other Santa did?"

"Oh yes. He walked up to the Santa in the chair and said something to him. There was nobody near them and the good Santa laughed at what the bad Santa said. I thought he'd told him a joke or something. Then the bad Santa went and stood next to the good Santa and I saw his lips move, and then his hand came up and he was holding something shiny in it. I didn't see what happened next because Mum grabbed my hand and told me we had to get going or we'd miss the bus home, so I turned and followed her. We were standing at the lift doors waiting for them to open when somebody screamed. After that, lots of people were running around and shouting and then the man in the grey uniform told us and everyone else that we had to stay here until the police came."

"Thank you Maisie," Curtis said, realising that Maisie had virtually given him a precise description of the murder. He was glad the poor kid hadn't seen the actual killing of Danny Thomas. She didn't need a memory like that in her mind at ten years of age. He liked the accuracy of her description of events, including the man in a grey uniform, obviously Pearson's own security guard. "I'll just go and have a word with my boss and we'll see about getting you and your Mum home. Is that okay with you?"

"Oh, yes, please. Will I get a ride in a police car?"

"Maybe," Curtis replied, and then left Maisie and her mother looking at a display of electronic games while he reported what she's told him to Ross, who had arrived on the shop floor after speaking to Edwin Pearson in his office.

Ross next had Izzie and Sam group everyone together so he could address than all together. Conversations with Izzie, Sam Gable, Ginger Devenish and Nick Dodds proved that four other people had seen the second Santa Claus. A word with Pearson revealed that the job of playing Santa Claus involved long hours at the minimum wage and it was therefore highly unlikely that someone had killed Danny Thomas from jealousy at not getting the job, though Ross refused to rule anything out at that stage.

Ross asked if anyone could tell them anything at all about the second Santa, apart from the fact he wore a red Santa suit of course. One girl, Ruth Mason, fourteen, perhaps a little more observant than most, had seen the second Santa too, and like Carrie Poole, had witnessed the man exiting through the doors that led to the stairs, and eventually of course, the exit. Ruth however, had one more piece of information that was of great interest to Ross.

"When he went through the doors, I could see he had a limp, and I saw an elf waiting for him."

"An elf?" Ross thought this case was getting stranger by the minute.

"Yes," Ruth insisted, "an elf, and even though I only saw them for a second before the doors swung shut, I'm sure the elf gave Santa a kiss."

"Okay," said Ross. "Thanks for that, Ruth. I'm sure it will be very helpful for us to know that."

Having taken statements from all the staff and customers, concentrating on those who had been on the second floor at the time of the murder, and having recorded the names and addresses of everyone in the store, Ross decided there was little to be gained by keeping everyone from going home and so released them all, having first warned them that they may be required to give further statements in the near future if the police required them.

"Er, sir," Tony Curtis said to his boss, after Ross announced that everyone could leave.

"What is it Tony?"

"It's young Maisie Poole. I almost, sort of promised that after coming forward with her information about the man she called the 'Bad Santa', I'd see if I could arrange a ride home for her and her Mum in a police car. I thought, with it being Christmas and all, and her being a good citizen, despite being only ten years old…"

"Say no more, Tony," Ross replied and called the two constables who'd been assisting him and his team on the second floor and instructed them to drive Carrie and Maisie Poole home, after which they could return to their normal duties for the remainder of their shift. Curtis indicated Maisie and her Mum to the two constables, and watched as they walked across and spoke to Carrie. The constables escorted Maisie and her mum to the lift doors and one officer pressed the call button. Just as the doors opened, however, little Maisie broke away from her Mum and the officers and ran across to where Curtis and Ross were standing. Before Tony Curtis could say or do anything, little Maisie Poole jumped up and he instinctively reacted by catching the little girl in his arms.

"Thank you," Maisie said, as she wrapped her arms around Curtis's neck and proceeded to plant a big, rather sloppy kiss on his right cheek. I can't believe I'm getting a ride in a police car. All my friends will be so jealous. It's the best Christmas present, *ever.*"

His face having turned a bright red, Tony Curtis gave the little girl a hug and gently lowered her to the floor. Beside him, he saw his boss grinning broadly and a quick look around allowed him to see similar looks on the faces of his colleagues.

"That's okay, Maisie. I did say I'd try, didn't I? This is my boss, Detective Inspector Ross, and he's the man who said it's okay for you and your mum to get a ride home in the police car."

Before he could react, Ross was the next one to be on the receiving end of Maisie's gratitude as she wrapped her arms around his legs and voiced her thanks to him as well.

"For a bizzie, you're a really nice man," she said. "Thank you too, and I hope you catch that bad Santa soon. Please be nice to Mr. Curtis at Christmas, won't you? He was so kind when he talked to me."

"Of course I will, Maisie," Ross spoke through his own embarrassment at the gushing thanks he was receiving from the little girl. "And I'm always nice to my detectives, especially at Christmas, isn't that right, D.C. Curtis."

"Oh yes, of course he is," Cutis said to Maisie, with a quick wink, and she replied with a conspiratorial grin.

"Come on Maisie," her Mum was calling, as one of the uniformed constables held lift doors open, preventing them from automatically closing. "These nice officers need to get back to work. They haven't got all night to wait for you, you know."

"Gotta go, bye, bye," Maisie shouted to Curtis and Ross and like a little four feet tall whirlwind, she skipped across the shop floor to her mum, took a hold of her hand and as the lift doors closed, she was last seen waving a frantic goodbye to Tony Curtis and Andy Ross, and then, she was gone.

"Well, well," Ross was grinning from ear to ear, "I think you've got a real fan there, Tony."

"Yes," Nick Dodds, who had sidled over to join them, agreed. "Not quite your type though, I'd have thought, mate. You usually prefer them just a few years older, don't you?" He laughed and Curtis reached across and gave his friend a playful slap across the back of his head.

"Sod off, you perv," he laughed. "I'll have you now young Maisie there is a very important witness and I'm glad I got to meet her. She's a lovely kid and unlike most of the kids nowadays, she really seems to have some respect for us, the police, I mean."

"Okay, let's get serious, people. We have a Santa and an elf to catch," Ross said, and, realising how ridiculous that sounded he slapped himself on the forehead and said, "What the hell did I just say?"

Nick Dodds began to answer, "Er, Boss, you said…"

"I know what I said, Nick. Now all we have to do is work out how and where to look for our two suspects. We can hardly get George

Thompson to put out a press release, saying, *Police are asking the public to be on the lookout for a Santa Claus with a limp and an elf, wanted in connection with the murder of another Santa Claus in Pearson's Emporium,* can we?"

George Thompson was the Press Liaison Officer at headquarters and would surely get a laugh out of trying to put a press information pack about this weird and very odd case.

"Don't let anyone see you loading a dead Santa into the van," Ross said to his old friend, Miles Booker as he and his techs prepared to ferry the dead man's body to the city mortuary. Can you imagine the flack we'd get if people, kids especially, thought Santa was dead?"

"No problem, Andy. I'll make sure he's safe from prying eyes," Booker promised.

"What about Danny Thomas's wife, sir?" Sam Gable asked. "Who gets to pay her a visit and ruin her Christmas?"

"I think under the circumstances, Izzie and I ought to do it. It is nearly Christmas and I think a senior officer, rather than a couple of constables ought to pay her a visit. The rest of you get yourselves home and unless something comes up between now and then, we'll meet in the briefing room at seven in the morning. A good early start might help us wrap this case up quickly, if we can get lucky."

Chapter 4

Good Santa, Bad Santa

By the time Ross and Drake pulled up outside the address of Danny Thomas in Wavertree that Edwin Pearson had provided them with, it was late, very late and midnight would be chiming very soon. As Drake pulled up in her car behind her boss, she took a few seconds to hope he'd like the Christmas present she and her husband Peter Foster had bought for him for Christmas, after consulting with his wife Maria. Izzie had retained her maiden name for work purposes when she and Peter, who was an administrator at the city mortuary, married two years previously. The pair of tickets for Everton's home game on New Year's Day against Tottenham Hotspur were in her handbag on the seat beside her. Though Maria Ross was definitely not a football fan, she would happily accompany her Everton supporting husband to the game as following his team was Ross's one passion outside of his work and she knew it would mean a lot to him to have her with him at the match.

Ross, meanwhile, had been rehearsing his words to the newly widowed Mrs. Thomas as he'd driven the few miles to her home. All he knew about her from her husband's employer was her name, Denise.

"Ready?" he asked as Izzie walked up to join him.

"As ready as it's possible to be. I hate these occasions," she replied.

"Let's get on with it then," Ross said as he led the way through the green painted garden gate and up the narrow path that led to the front door of the Thomas's home. The downstairs lights were on, and both police officers assumed Mrs. Thomas would be siting or maybe pacing anxiously, wondering why her husband was so late in coming home from work. Even with the lounge curtains drawn, they were able to make out the twinkling of coloured lights, presumably from a Christmas tree, in the main room of the house.

Ross looked for a doorbell, couldn't see one, so knocked firmly and loudly on the door. It was opened within a few seconds by a woman who appeared considerably younger than Danny Thomas. Denise Thomas had to be at least ten years younger than her husband, and Ross's senses began twitching for some reason.

"Mrs Denise Thomas?" he asked, just to be sure he had the right woman.

"Yes. How can I help you at this time of night?" she replied, but didn't appear unduly phased by a stranger knocking on her front door late at night.

Ross held up his warrant card, as did Drake, standing beside him.

"I'm Detective Inspector Drake, and this is Detective Sergeant Drake. We're here about your husband, Daniel."

"Yes, what about him? What's he done?" Denise asked.

"Perhaps we could come in and sit down, Mrs. Thomas, rather than stand talking on the doorstep."

"Yes, okay," she replied and led them into the lounge, where the Christmas tree lights twinkled cheerfully in one corner and a large screen TV was showing a late-night movie in another corner. The one big incongruity as far as Ross and Drake were concerned was the well-dressed man, seated on the sofa, looking for all the world as if he was perfectly at home in the house of Daniel Thomas. Ross instinctively knew something wasn't right about the picture he was seeing here.

"Now, what do you want to tell me about Danny?" Denise Thomas asked. "Oh, don't mind Charlie. He's Danny's brother. He's staying with us at the moment."

Denise walked to the sofa and sat down at the opposite corner to Charlie.

"Oh, I see," Ross replied, but his senses were twitching. "I'm afraid I have bad news, Mrs. Thomas. Earlier this evening, your husband, Daniel Thomas, was stabbed and killed while at his place of work in Pearson's Emporium."

"What? Danny? Surely not, you must be mistaken."

Ross felt that the words were right but they lacked emotion.

"There's no mistake, I'm afraid," Ross continued. "Your husband was working as a Santa Claus for Pearson's, am I right?"

"Yes, but..."

"Then there's no mistake. We're going to have to ask you to identify the body officially of course, but that can wait until tomorrow."

Denise Thomas seemed at a loss for words, and Izzie Drake decided to play a hunch. She surreptitiously winked at Ross, who seemed to realise she was about to try something.

"This must have come as a shock to you, Mrs. Thomas. Perhaps we could all do with a nice cup of tea. Mr. Thomas, Charlie, maybe you can help me in the kitchen while D.I. Ross talks with your sister-in-law?"

"What? Oh yeah, right, sure," Charlie Thomas said, having not said a word previously, even at the news of his brother's murder.

Charlie Thomas rose from the sofa as Izzie got up from the chair in which she was sitting, and as she went to follow him into the kitchen, both she and Ross couldn't fail to notice the limp with which Danny Thomas's brother walked. Ross nodded at Drake and also stood. "Got a bad leg, have you, Mr. Thomas?"

"What? On yes, I was in a car accident as a boy and it got broken in two places. Never healed right and left me with the limp."

"But you can get around alright, I take it?"

"Well, yeah."

"Have you been out tonight, either of you?" Ross's investigative antennae were now on full alert. He was like a shark on the prowl, and he could sense blood in the water.

"No, we've been here all evening, watching telly,"

"What have you been watching?" Drake asked.

The couple looked at each other. Denise replied, "Oh well, a bit of this and that, you know?"

"No, we don't know. Why don't you tell us?" Ross pressed them for an answer. When they both fell silent, Drake asked Denise,

"Come on, Mrs. Thomas. Lets go and put that kettle on."

Relived to escape the cauldron of pressure her own lounge had become, Denise Thomas followed Izzie as she went in search of the kitchen. As soon as she walked in to the room, Izzie Drake's eyes locked on the knife block that stood on the kitchen counter. She immediately saw that one knife was missing.

"Why don't you tell us the truth, Denise? We're not idiots, you know."

"I don't know what you mean," Denise replied.

"Oh, I think you do," Drake insisted. "I see you have a knife missing. What's the betting, when we check it, we'll find the knife that killed your husband is the one that matches the ones in your knife block?"

Denise Thomas started to cry. It was obvious that neither she nor her brother-in-law were in any way professional killers. Whatever happened had to have been a spur of the moment thing.

"We're in love," Denise suddenly said, sniffing as the tears began to flow. Me and Charlie, we just wanted to go away together, but Charlie's got no money and Danny would never have let me go."

While Denise let it all come out, Izzie quietly removed her handcuffs from her bag and before Denise knew it, Drake had snapped the cuffs in place.

Drake led Denise into the lounge where she was happy to see that Ross had also restrained Charlie Thomas.

"The Santa suit and the elf costume are in his car, the blue Astra parked on the street," Ross said as he smiled at the sight of Denise Thomas in handcuffs.

"There's a knife missing from the block in the kitchen," Drake confirmed. "Seems we have a love triangle and poor old Danny ended up as the loser," she said.

"Poor sod," Ross exclaimed. "Wy did you have to kill him? Couldn't you just have left him?" he asked the wife.

"She says they couldn't afford to go," Drake answered instead.

Ross just shook his head. People never ceased to amaze him.

"Call it in, please, Izzie. Let's get these two tucked up into a couple of nice, cosy cells for the night."

"Right boss," said Drake, taking her mobile phone out and quickly called for back-up. It wasn't long before a police car arrived outside and two uniformed officers arrived to transport the pair to police head-quarters, where they'd spend the night before being formally interviewed and charged in the morning.

"The team will get a nice surprise in the morning," she said to Ross as they prepared to part and drive home in their own cars.

"They sure will," Ross agreed. "You just never know what you're going to find when you go to inform a widow of her husband's death, do you?"

Drake smiled and pulled her car door open. She turned to her boss, and wished him goodnight.

"Goodnight, Izzie," Ross replied. "Don't be late in the morning."

Chapter 5

Merry Christmas

The morning briefing certainly wasn't what most of the Special Murder Investigation Squad were expecting. Those who'd attended the previous night's call out were stunned to learn that Ross and Drake had not only solved the case but had the two killers in custody too. Those who hadn't even known about the call-out were full of admiration for Ross and Drake though Ross stressed they'd been lucky to come across two of the most inept murderers they'd ever known.

"It's been an eventful year, people, but we've come through it with the team intact and no disasters. Well done everyone, and Tony, special well done for the way you handled young Maisie last night. She not only helped solve the murder but you helped to make that little girl's Christmas really special."

"Thanks, Boss," Curtis said, "I was just doing my job."

"And a bit more, I think," Ross winked at his detective, who would spend most of the morning explaining to his colleagues just what he'd done the previous night.

The squadroom door opened to admit Detective Chief Inspector Oscar Agostini. In overall control of the squad, Agostini had come down from is office, having just read the overnight crime reports and seen the details of last night's operation.

"Morning all," he said, cheerfully. "I understand congratulations are in order, Andy. That must be some kind of record, even for you lot of super cops. Called out and crime solved, perpetrators in custody within 4 hours. Not bad, not bad at all."

Agostini clapped his D.I. and his sergeant, and unbidden, the rest of the team joined in until the squad room resounded with the sound of applause. Ross and Drake blushed and gracefully accepted the congratulations of their colleagues, before Ross spoke.

"We got lucky, that's all, sir. It wasn't really a Special Murder Squad case, I just happened to be the officer on call for the evening. It could have been a robbery, a fire, anything really."

"Don't be modest, Andy. The call couldn't have fallen to a better man, and woman, D.S. Drake. You moved quickly and cleared the whole thing up in no time. Not every officer on the force could have done it."

"Okay, I know when I'm beat," said Ross. "On behalf of me and Izzie, thank you all, and as we're only two days away from Christmas, the drinks are on me after work, usual place. You've all worked hard and it's the least I can do."

"Oh no, you won't, D.I. Ross," a female voice spoke up from the rear of the squad room. Nobody had noticed Detective Chief Superintendent Sarah Hollingsworth, who headed up the detective division within police headquarters, enter the room. "I've also heard about last night's exploits and the drinks are on me, ladies and gentlemen. I'm damn proud to have you all on my team, and I'm also standing the Specialist Murder Squad down for three days after we finish today. Unless there's a really dire case that requires your special expertise, you're all on leave until December 27th. If any of you already have leave booked over the holidays, you'll be credited for those three days. These are my own way of thanking you all for your work in the last twelve months."

A stunned silence filled the room for about three seconds, until Ross himself began a round of applause, which was taken up by the rest of the team, and he managed to mouth, "Thank you ma'am," to the D.C.S. before she quietly left the room.

"Well, everyone, I guess that just about wraps things up for us. Izzie and I are going to talk to Denise and Charlie Thomas about her husband's murder, but, being as how neither of them is what we might call a career criminal, it shouldn't take long to get the facts from them, even if they have a solicitor appointed. The rest of you clear your paperwork, Paul, make sure the computer files are updated to include last night's case. We might as well add it to our list of successful investigations, then you and Kat close down for the holidays."

Sergeant Paul Ferris, the team's computer genius, and admin assistant Kat Bellamy, who worked closely with him, soon had everything up to date and were ready to switch off in order to begin the Christmas holidays.

Sam Gable caught Ross's attention.

"I won't be able to stay too long at the pub, sir. I'm heading off to Oldham to stay with Ian for the holidays."

During a recent investigation, Sam had worked with a member of the Greater Manchester Police Force, Detective Sergeant Ian Gilligan and the two had struck up a romantic relationship. Ross was happy for Sam.

"No need to apologise, Sam. Just leave when you have to, and have a great time with Ian."

"Thanks, Boss," she smiled and gave Ross a kiss on the cheek.

As the time came for them to leave for a welcome session at the pub, Ross took a quick look around the almost silent squad room. For once, their was no banter flowing backwards and forwards across the room, no sounds of fingers busily tapping on keyboards, or the sounds of voices speaking into telephones on the mostly deserted desks. Ross walked across to the large plate glass window that looked out over the station car park, and saw light snow flurries blowing in the wind, adding a feeling of peace and Christmas goodwill to his thoughts. He gave a last thought to the two killers of Danny Thomas, the innocent victim of the Santa Claus murder, who now resided in cells until they could be remanded to jail awaiting trial. Their ill thought-out plan that they hoped would lead them to a future together would probably result in them never seeing each other again, after their trial and convictions.

A tap on his shoulder brought him out of his solitary reverie. It was Izzie Drake.

"You ready to go?" she asked.

"Definitely," he replied. "Let's go, the D.C.S.'s money is burning a hole in my pocket and I need a drink."

An hour later, as the drinks flowed and the pub was filling up, and Ross's team were getting into the Christmas spirit, with jokes and laughter abounding, Sergeant Bob Willis, an old friend of Ross's who'd been on the headquarters reception desk that day, walked up to the group. For a minute, Ross had the awful feeling that another job had come up.

"I'm looking for D.C. Curtis," Willis shouted above the din.

"Over here, Sarge," Curtis called from his place behind Ginger Devenish, just out of Willis's line of sight. Everyone fell silent for a minute, wondering what this was all about. Willis was holding a large white envelope in his hand, and a small, poorly wrapped package, in gaudy Christmas wrapping paper.

"I just had a visit from a young lady," Willis said. "She wanted to be sure these reached Detective Constable Curtis. She said she couldn't wait, because her mum was waiting outside and they needed to go visit her gran. She said her name was Maisie and you'd know who she is."

Willis passed the envelope and the package to Curtis, who, with a lump in his throat, accepted them from the desk sergeant. He quickly opened up the small package and there, inside was a little tiny teddy bear which he sat on the table in front of him. Turning his attention to the envelope, he carefully opened it and removed a large Christmas card with a big picture of Santa Claus on the front. Opening the card, he read the words and then, with everyone watching and waiting, he read Maisie Poole's words, written by the hand of a ten-year old little girl.

Detective Constable Curtis, thank you for believing me when nobody else would. I hope I helped you catch the bad Santa. You are a very nice policeman, even my Mum said so. And thank you for keeping your promise to get me a ride home in a police car. It was so exciting. I used to be a bit scared of the police, but after last night I think you are all very nice. I know I told you that teddy bears are for little kids, but this one has sat on my dressing table since I was very small and I thought you might like it to bring you good luck and to remember me by. You could call it Maisie. Your friend, Maisie Poole, XXXXXXXXXX.

Tony Curtis paused for a second to clear the even bigger lump that had formed in his throat, and to wipe away the beginnings of an emotional tear that threatened to destroy his macho image. Then, he read the final two words in Maisie's card...MERRY CHRISTMAS.

Dear reader,

We hope you enjoyed reading *A Merry Mersey Christmas*. Please take a moment to leave a review, even if it's a short one. Your opinion is important to us.

Discover more books by Brian L. Porter at https://www.nextchapter.pub/authors/brian-porter-mystery-author-liverpool-united-kingdom

Want to know when one of our books is free or discounted? Join the newsletter at http://eepurl.com/bqqB3H

Best regards,

Brian L. Porter and the Next Chapter Team

The Author

Brian L Porter is an award-winning author, whose books have also regularly topped the Amazon Best Selling charts, fifteen of which have to date been Amazon bestsellers. Most recently, the third book in his Mersey Mystery series, *A Mersey Maiden* was voted The Best Book We've Read This Year, 2018, by the organisers and readers of Read-free.ly.

A Mersey Mariner was voted the Top Crime Novel in the Top 50 Best Indie Books, 2017 awards, while *Sheba: From Hell to Happiness* won the Best Nonfiction section and also won the Preditors & Editors Best Nonfiction Book Award, 2017. Writing as Brian, he has won a Best Author Award, a Poet of the Year Award, and his thrillers have picked up Best Thriller and Best Mystery Awards.

His short story collection *After Armageddon* is an international bestseller and his moving collection of remembrance poetry, *Lest We Forget*, is also an Amazon best seller.

Three rescue dogs, three bestsellers!

In a recent departure from his usual thriller writing, Brian has written three successful books about three of the eleven rescued dogs who share his home, with more to follow.

Sasha, A Very Special Dog Tale of a Very Special Epi-Dog is now an international bestseller and winner of the Preditors & Editors Best Nonfiction Book, 2016, and was placed 7th in The Best Indie Books of 2016, and *Sheba: From Hell to Happiness* is a UK #1 bestseller, and award winner as detailed above. Earlier in 2018, Cassie's Tale was released and instantly became the best-selling new release in its category on Amazon in the USA.

If you love dogs, you'll love these three offerings which will soon be followed by book 4 in the series *Saving Dylan.*

Writing as Harry Porter his children's books have achieved three bestselling rankings on Amazon in the USA and UK.

In addition, his third incarnation as romantic poet Juan Pablo Jalisco has brought international recognition with his collected works, *Of Aztecs and Conquistadors* topping the bestselling charts in the USA, UK and Canada.

Brian lives with his wife, children and a wonderful pack of eleven rescued dogs. He is also the in-house screenwriter for ThunderBall Films, (L.A.), for whom he is also a co-producer on a number of their current movie projects.

The Mersey Mysteries have already been optioned for TV/movie adaptation, in addition to his other novels, all of which have been signed by ThunderBall Films in a movie franchise deal.

Look out for the 7th book in the Mersey Mystery series, *The Mersey Monastery Murders*, coming soon.

See Brian's website at http://www.brianlporter.co.uk/

His blog is at https://sashaandharry.blogspot.co.uk/

You might also like:

A Mersey Killing by Brian L. Porter

To read the first chapter for free, please head to:
https://www.nextchapter.pub/books/mersey-killing-british-crime-
mystery

A Merry Mersey Christmas
ISBN: 978-4-86747-096-1

Published by
Next Chapter
1-60-20 Minami-Otsuka
170-0005 Toshima-Ku, Tokyo
+818035793528
14th May 2021

CPSIA information can be obtained
at www.ICGtesting.com
Printed in the USA
LVHW022056310521
689000LV00007B/407